The Collapse

Tales from *Perfect Pond*

CONNIE JOHNSON

About the Series

Tales from Perfect Pond is a series of novelettes written by American author Connie Johnson. The stories record the lives of seven protectors with godlike powers who are trying to prevent their enemy from wreaking havoc on their lives.

The Collapse changes everything for Classie Jones. When an angry storm collapses a wooden bridge on her family's ranch, Classie Jones and Jake Mercy, her husband, are launched into a rushing creek. After fighting for her life, Classie finds Mercy unconscious. When Mercy wakes, the unthinkable has happened. He's paralyzed and insists that Classie leave him for dead. What Classie doesn't realize is her decision to save his life will change their lives forever.

COPYRIGHT

This book is a work of fiction. Names, characters, places, and incidents are the product of the author's imagination or are used fictitiously. Any resemblance to actual events, locales, or persons, living or dead, is coincidental.

This book contains adult content.

Connie Johnson Publishing
Printed in the United States of America
First trade edition: October 2021
Paperback edition ISBN: 9798486843549

Acknowledgments

I'm blessed to call my editor, Georgia Griffith Helton, my friend. Thank you for your challenging work.

I'm blessed to be surrounded by family and friends who continue to support me. I love you, Jeff Johnson, Makayla Perry, and Asher Perry.

I acknowledge that Jesus Christ is my Lord. His grace, mercy, and love endure forever. Amen.

Dedication

This book is dedicated to those who believe fantasy can become our reality.

"For we wrestle not against flesh and blood, but against principalities, against powers, against the rulers of the darkness of this world, against spiritual wickedness in high places." Ephesians 6:12

Introduction

Tales from Perfect Pond

Numerous times we crossed the wooden creek bridge on our recreational vehicles, but this time was deadly. Channel 8 News forecast flash flooding, gusty winds, and possible hail. The forecast was accurate, as a vicious thunderstorm moved in at noon. Heavy rain poured down while lightning bolted across the Texas sky.

The Collapse

He was in control, and I was on the back holding tight with my arms around his waist. As we approached the wooden bridge at a high rate of speed, he slowed down to observe the crossing, which was blocked by debris.

After removing the debris, he noticed that I was holding my stomach. He fought the gusty wind to return to me.

"I'm not well," I declared and dismounted from the vehicle.

"This storm is worsening. It's definitely an angry one," he said and gently kissed my lips. "Your olive complexion is white as a white rose, and your health is withering away, like a rose in a vase left without water."

I grew worse as the darkness clouded my vision.

He pointed to a cone-shaped funnel cloud. "Let's go!" he screamed.

"No. It's not safe. We won't make it across the bridge. The water level is too high."

But in a blink of an eye, he cradled me in his arms, and gently placed me back on the vehicle.

"Hold on tight," he said.

We raced across the bridge, but halfway across it, the vehicle stalled out.

Snap!

Crackle!

Pop!

The bridge collapsed.

Perfect Pond

I'm depressed thinking about why I'm standing at the entrance of an amusement park in San Antonio, Texas, in a white sun dress and canvas shoes, waiting on my date to arrive.

For the last three years, I have played out the collapse of the bridge in my mind and the craziness that followed it. But I'm exhausted fighting my poor mental state of mind. So today, I'm hoping for a breakthrough. I'm hoping to meet a man who will make me feel like I'm alive.

When I see his outward appearance, my hope vanishes. He's not my type. He's tall and lanky wearing a white polo shirt, khaki cargo shorts, and slip-on canvas shoes. "Hello," he says.

I swallow hard. "Doug," I say with disappointment, "Your hair is brighter in person than in your pictures."

"A redheaded man has less of a chance getting prostate cancer," he gently says with a beautiful smile.

"True. But you're more likely to be attacked by a bee. They perceive your hair color as a threat."

He laughs, and then pays the cashier for our tickets. "What would you like to ride first?" he asks and hands me a ticket.

"A roller coaster."

His friendly demeanor quickly changes. "When I was married to my ex-wife, I felt like I was on a roller coaster. Up and down. Hot and cold. In and out. Can you choose a different ride?"

As we wait in line to eat, Doug gestures towards a woman and asks, "Do you see that nice looking woman over there? How about we ask her to join us for a threesome?"

His disrespect for me immediately has me remembering everything my father taught me about men. "If you learn from your mistakes, you can always improve yourself. The key to life is to show mercy," he said. My father taught me not only about making mistakes and showing mercy to others, but also about life and the people in it, by comparing them to fish, flies, and pond creatures, while fishing at the pond on our ranch. He was preparing me for womanhood. His goal was for me to catch myself a trophy bass.

I turned ten when we began our first fishing lesson.

"This is your birthday gift from me," he said.

I tore open the yellow gift box and held up a pair of yellow rain boots and frowned. I was disappointed with his gift.

"What's wrong?" he asked.

"These boots are yellow."

"It's time to fish. We'll talk about the boots later."

I sat next to him and watched him rig my pole. "I'm thankful to God, my girl, that he created you to be a quiet child. You're the perfect fishing partner. This pond needs perfect fishermen."

"This pond isn't perfect. The water is stinky and muddy." I glared at the muddy water. "I can't see my fishing line!"

"Yes, my girl, the water is stinky and muddy. But—can you see the beautiful nature surrounding the pond?" He pointed at the green lily pads that were floating. "There's a reason that I bought you these yellow rain boots. The boots will protect you from the messiness of the pond while you enjoy the beauty of it." He squeezed the toe of the boot. "See? These are made from rubber and will protect you from creatures like snakes."

I looked at the yellow boots for a solid moment. "But I hate yellow!"

"Do you see those yellow water lilies on the green lily pad?"

I focused on the lilies. "Yep!"

"Those are called Texas Dawn lilies. See how vivid and bright the yellow petals are? Yellow like the sun. The sun generates warmth. When you see yellow think about the warmth of the sun and try and think positive thoughts. Never let your negative thoughts outweigh your positive ones. Now, get up. Wade into the pond and smell those Texas Dawn lilies."

I was knee high to a grasshopper in my new yellow rain boots as I waded to the lily. I leaned over and put my nose to it, but a frog jumped up and scared me to death. "Oh, Lord!" I screamed, "That darn ole' frog got me."

Dad laughed so hard that he fell out of his folded chair.

"Daddy, are you alright?"

"I'm fine. That frog got you good." He sat the folding chair back up as I returned to him. Then he gently scolded me. "Do not use God's name in vain. It's disrespectful."

I pouted.

"Did you smell the lily before the frog jumped on you?"

"Yep, it smells like a sour ole' lemon."

"The theory behind a lemon scent is that it can energize the body. A lemon is what color?" he asked.

"Yellow."

"Just like the lily. Just like the sun. When you see yellow let it create a feeling of joy inside of you. God's creation, although it appears to be ugly to us, is perfect to him. Therefore, I call this place Perfect Pond. It has all the qualities that God requires it to have to make it perfect. All things are beautiful if we choose to see the beauty in them."

My stomach growled. "I'm hungry."

"Bring us the sandwiches that you made. They're in the picnic basket in the back of my truck."

I ran over to the truck and opened the picnic basket and removed two sandwiches.

But Dad noticed his sandwich had mustard running out of it. "This sandwich is messy. Let us try and make it neater next time."

I bit into my sandwich. "No. It just appears to be messy. I see it as a beautiful creation. See?" I pointed at his sandwich. "The mustard is yellow. Just like the lily. Just like the sun. Just like the lemon. Allow it to create a feeling of joy inside of you." I shrugged my shoulders. "What can I say? I learn fast." I gulped down a bottled water, and then tossed it in the back of the truck. "You know what this water is missing?" I asked.

"No. What?"

I put my hands on my hips. Sassy and spunky, I replied, "A sour ole' lemon."

He gave me a hug. "You sure do catch on quick. Let us go sit under the cabana in the shade." He carried the fishing poles to the bench under the cabana.

He cast.

I cast.

He reeled.

I reeled.

But the fish weren't biting.

I tossed my pole down at his feet. "Why aren't we catching any fish?"

"Be patient. This pond is stocked with plenty of fish. You'll catch one." He picked up my pole and gave it back. "But you're not going to catch one if you give up. Never give up. You're a Jones. We never quit."

So, I cast again.

"My girl, this pond has catfish, minnows, goldfish, and bass. I'm going to teach you about these fish. This will make you an excellent fisherman. There is no better place to teach you about fish than here at the pond. When you hear the word fish, I want you to think about boys."

"Boys?" I asked, my voice loud.

"Yes. Boys. Keep your voice down. Remember? The perfect fishing partner is quiet." He baited his hook. "It's time to discuss boys."

I jumped off the bench. "Let me get this right. You want me to talk about boys?"

"Yes."

I plopped back down. "I don't need to talk about boys. I know all I need to know about them."

He displayed an uncertain look on his face. "Is that so?"

"Yep, that's so." I bent over and cupped some pond water. I raised it to my nose and breathed it in. "Boys are stinky like this here water." Then I let the water run out of my hands.

Dad shook his head and grinned. "In two or three years you'll start noticing boys. Your mother will teach you how to catch one. But it is my job to teach you about the types of boys you can catch."

I wiped my hands on my coveralls and insisted, "I'm not going to catch a boy!"

He removed a silver, slippery fish from the pond. He hooked it in the mouth and blood ran out of its body. I was a bit squeamish at the site of the blood. "This is a minnow. Listen closely to what I have to say about them. Every creature that God creates has positive and negative things about it. The minnow is a sociable fish. It's an alive, mobile, active fish. Mobile Minnows is a good name for them. They're defenders, too. The negative thing about a minnow is that it's small. Other bigger fish can swallow them whole even though they try hard to defend their territory."

I eyeballed the hook. "Oh my, they're bait."

"Yes, they're bait. The point I'm trying to make with this is that these fish defend their homes. They're fun to be around too even though they're small."

"Daddy, they're fish. They can't be fun."

He stared icily at me. "Boys not fish. We are talking about boys."

I rolled my eyes.

He used the minnow as bait and reeled in a dusky, gray fish with whiskers. He kept the fish in the water and used his heel to prevent it from moving. "Catfish swim at the bottom of the pond. The pond enjoys having a catfish around because they help keep it clean. The negatives however outweigh the positives. These bottom-feeders are commonly naked and aren't picky. They will eat and touch anything. They would rather sink than float with no real ambition. If they become irritated, they can harm you. You're bound to catch a catfish."

I pointed at the catfish while kneeling by it. The catfish moved when he released his heel. I jumped up and shouted, "Yuck! They have ugly whiskers."

He grinned. "I hope that you don't catch one of these in life, but you probably will. They're players with those whiskers. A cheating catfish is not a fish you want to keep." He released the catfish from his hook and tossed it back in the pond. "Let's discuss a fish that isn't in our pond." He put his hands on my shoulders and stared into my eyes. "Under no circumstances do you want to ever catch or keep a fish that you can't identify. If it conceals its identity by modifying its appearance, it's dangerous. If you catch one by mistake, then cut it from your line quickly. Release it!"

I shrugged my shoulders. "What if the fish fears getting caught? If I were a fish, I wouldn't want a hook in my mouth. That could be why it conceals its identity."

"That's exactly right. If they're concealing their identity, it's for a reason. My hope for you is that you catch a fish that wants to be caught."

"Okay, daddy. I'll throw it back if I catch one."

He changed out his bait.

I looked intently at the hook. "You're using a beautiful bug."

"This is a dragonfly. We will talk about flies, bugs, and insects later. Every fisherman wants a trophy fish. It's the only reason we go fishing. The largemouth bass is a trophy fish. This fish is so big it can feed the family. Bass will consume a variety of things, so they're easy to cook for. They're fighters. They're survivors. Burly bass are well-rounded fish. I want you to catch a burly bass."

I was confused. "This fishing thing is really hard to understand. I don't know if I'm going to remember all this."

"The more experience you have fishing, the better you will become at catching. If you catch a fish look at it. Decide. Is it a keeper? Or do you want to throw it back in the pond? If it's a keeper, never throw it back. You don't want to chance another fisherman catching it."

"How will I know if it's a keeper?"

"The moment you catch a keeper you will know it when your face lights up with excitement. Do you understand?"

"Yep! Boys are fish. Fish are boys. Perfect Pond is the world."

"That's it exactly!"

I puckered my lips like a fish and said, "I am right. Boys are stinky. I never want to catch a stinky fish."

I look at Doug with confidence. "You're not right for me. Good luck at the bottom of the pond."

Hours later, to help me with my poor state of mind, I meet my best friend, Gianna, and her boyfriend, Matt, at a bar. When I walk inside, she motions for me to join them at a booth. "Good evening," I say to her with a frown.

"It didn't go that well, huh?" she asks, and then gestures towards a man sitting across from her. "Brett Rainey, this is my best friend, Classie Jones. She'll be joining us this evening."

He stands to greet me. His deep set, brown eyes, with long eyelashes, instantly catches my attention. His light all over beard, short brown hair, and masculine square face has been featured on *Sporting It Magazine.*

I survey his graphic James Dean t-shirt and blue jeans.

"Classie is a beautiful name," he says with a sultry, Southern drawl.

I glance over at Matt, refusing to believe who is standing in front of me. "This is Brett Rainey."

"I know," Matt replies. "I'm his sports agent."

I deal with the anxiety, from meeting the hottest male in sports, by taking a lot of air into my lungs.

"Please have a seat. And my name is just Rainey," he says and gestures for me to slide in next to him.

Gianna laughs lightly. "And you should exhale before Rainey has to give you CPR."

I blush, *thinking that would be alright by me.*

"Shall we order you a cocktail?" Matt asks with hesitation.

"No. Sweet tea for me."

"Do you not drink alcohol?" Rainey asks before he orders a beer.

"I'm driving to my hometown tomorrow. I'd rather not drive with a hangover."

"And where is your hometown?"

"Tye."

"That's not too far from where I play baseball."

"Good ole' baseball," I murmur.

"Classie has always wanted to know what it's like pitching for the Dallas Wardens," Gianna says with a giggle, knowing that I dislike the sport.

"Actually, I'm not much of a baseball fan."

"You dislike baseball?" Rainey asks looking at me as if I've wounded him. "But baseball is America's game."

"I'd have to disagree with you. I think most Americans like football."

Matt nonchalantly texts on his phone. "Well, I hate to break up this tiff over baseball, but Gianna and I have an appointment in the morning with another client." He slides out of the booth. "And it just so happens he used to play for America's team," he says with a wink.

"We have to leave right now?" Gianna asks and grabs her purse.

"I'm afraid so. It's important that I continue my conversation with him."

"My apologies to you and Rainey," Gianna says and gives me a hug.

Matt continues to text on his phone. "Classie, tomorrow I'm meeting my client at a lake house in Marble Falls. He's asked if you'd like to join us."

I glance briefly at Matt. "Are you talking about Jake Mercy?" I ask perturbed.

"I'm afraid so," he responds and then shakes Rainey's hand. "Rainey, if you need anything please give me a call. I'm certain your appointment with the surgeon will go well."

"You know I will," Rainey replies.

"And Classie, will I see you in Marble Falls tomorrow?" he asks and kisses me on the corner of my mouth.

I offer Matt my best smile. "I wouldn't miss an opportunity to see him again," I say and watch him exit the bar before I offer my hand to Rainey. "Brett, it was my pleasure."

"Just Rainey." He accepts my handshake.

"Rainey." And with a nod, I leave a trophy fish standing alone in a bar.

The Lake House

As I step out of my vehicle, in Marilyn Monroe style, I expose my toned abdominal muscles in a red crop top and white high waisted shorts and elevate my long legs in a pair of red wedge heels. I walk towards our lake house and smile at the breath-taking scenic view that Lake Marble Falls provides.

Gianna greets me at the entrance of the red stucco, two-story house hidden away from the world behind some large trees. "I'm glad you came," she says with a hint of excitement.

"Can you believe Bob Mercy, Mercy's grandfather, purchased this for us as a wedding gift?"

"No. I still can't believe you married him when you turned eighteen," she replies.

I push open the front door and step inside. "Let's see if he tells me the truth."

The décor hasn't changed. The living room has a high ceiling with walls painted in light yellow. It's furnished with two tan chairs and a matching couch that features light blue and light green designs. An old white Bible is sitting on the living room coffee table. I walk over to the coffee table and open the Bible. A bookmark marks a verse that's highlighted in yellow. I read, "Song of Songs 1:2: Let him kiss me with the kisses of his mouth! For your love is more delightful than wine."

"My favorite verse," a voice from behind me says.

I do an about face and stare into his blue eyes, and then I envision his alluring lips kissing me. "Mercy."

"Why do you call him by his last name?" Matt asks before offering me a glass of wine.

I wave off the glass. "Throughout school I was bullied by a girl named Jenny Taylor."

"For what?" Matt asks and places the wine glass on an end table.

"I had a speech impediment. That's another story. Anyways, after Jake Mercy moved to our high school and stood up to her, she stopped bullying me."

"Jenny had a crush on me," Mercy says and retrieves the wine glass from the end table. He throws it back.

"Rumor is she still has a crush on you!" I snap with jealousy. I calm my voice, "Matt, I call Mercy by his last name because he showed me some compassion in high school."

Matt laughs. "That's because he wanted to hit it. Look at you. You're hot!"

Mercy's eyes wash over my silhouette. "Would you like to talk in the master bedroom?" he asks.

With the Bible in my hand, I walk with him through the house until we reach the master suite.

The master suite has multiple sitting areas with large windows that surround it, generating natural light. A fireplace accents the room to provide warmth when used during a chilly winter.

I stare at the bed where a red satin comforter overlays its mattress. I run my hand over the satin. "How long has it been since?" I ask, searching his eyes for the truth.

He takes a step towards me.

"I'm listening," I say and sit on the edge of the bed.

"How long has it been since what?"

"Since you've made love to someone other than me on this bed?"

He clears his throat. "Last night."

I look at him as if he's a stranger to me. "Tell me about the girl you had sex with last night."

"No!"

I stand to exit the bedroom.

He grabs my upper arm. "I was standing at the edge of this bed when she walked out of the bathroom with nothing on." He pauses. "Shall I go on?" He gazes at my lips. "How long has it been since?" he asks with a seducing voice.

"How long has it been since what?"

He runs his finger along the bottom of my lip. "Since you've been kissed by someone other than me?"

Jacqueline Classie Jones

Three hours later, I approach the main entrance to Jones Ranch where a white iron-gate is newly landscaped with tan bricks. I follow the dirt road until it turns into pavement. I cross a cattle guard and drive around the circular driveway. I stare at my childhood home, a white stucco, two-story, seven-thousand-three hundred square feet, colonial style house, with four bedrooms and five bathrooms. There's a white pipe fence which is the perimeter that blocks off the main house from another sixty-eight acres. The property has a silver metal stable barn and storage building that sits on the east side. Jones Ranch is heavily treed with rolling hills, one-acre pond, and one five-acre lake.

I notice my sister's black car parked in the three-vehicle attached garage. She runs out of the guest house screaming, "Welcome home," and then embraces me.

"Not so tight, Norma," I say and push her away. "I need to breathe."

"But I'm excited you're home."

"Where's Tony?"

Tony Peterson, Norma's attorney husband, is sitting on a gold-colored couch in the guest house with his skinny legs propped up on an ottoman. "Nice to see you, Class," he says.

"What in the world has mom done with this place? The interior design has completely changed. The once rustic country interior is now white and modern. Please tell me that my bedroom hasn't changed?"

"Wish I could," Norma replies with a giggle.

"I've been gone from Tye for one year and mom has changed everything. Where's dad?"

"He's praying in his office."

"And mom?"

"At work."

To understand why my father is devoted to God, and why my mother is devoted to work, you must understand my family's history.

The Jones-Anderson families are a force to be reckoned with.

The Jones family was led by Jacob Jones Senior, my great-grandfather, who died at the age of fifty-five from an apparent heart attack. Heart attacks run in the Jones family. And every Jones man that has died has left their children with millions of dollars. History handed Jacob Jones Junior, my grandfather, that inheritance.

Jacob Jones Junior married, my grandmother, Rose Rodgers Jones. They bought land in the small town of Tye Town. It was there they founded Jones Ranch. It was there Rose gave birth to John Jones, my father.

But Rose passed away from an unknown illness when my father was six years old. She had a bit of a free spirit, a gypsy side and rumors circulated throughout Tye Town that she had a scandalous affair that somehow led to her death.

But my father didn't allow his mother's death to control him. His father raised him to be a Christian man regardless of life's circumstances. He was determined to use Jones money to further his education and build a fortune of his own. He was accepted to a Texas university where he pursued a degree in Agriculture.

Julie Anderson, my mother, was an eldest child, raised by Andrew, a bank loan officer, and Traci, a homemaker. The Andersons were a middle-class family. Money was rare, but it didn't prevent my grandfather from saving for her college fund. His savings paid off when my mother enrolled into the same college as my father.

Her creative, artistic, and intelligent abilities helped her pursue a business degree. She had an eye for detail. She loved fashion. She loved designing. Her fashion influences were Jacqueline Kennedy Onassis and Marilyn Monroe. But it was Jacqueline Kennedy's style that transformed her life.

She was invited to attend a Fourth of July event at a local church. She wore a red, neck tie, shift dress with Jackie O sunglasses. It was that dress that caught the eye of my father.

They developed a strong friendship which later blossomed into a romantic relationship. Mom loved that my dad was a polite and honest man. Dad loved my mom’s zeal for life.

After they graduated from college, Dad proposed to Mom on the Fourth of July. They had their preacher marry them at the same small church where they met. It was a simple wedding with just their parents. And Dad became the pastor of that church seven years later and named it Perfect Pond.

Mom started a real estate-interior design business with the financial backing of her father-in-law. The business prospered quickly. It allowed her to build her own financial wealth. With wealth, came clothes and the style she dreamed about most of her life, but an unexpected pregnancy shook the world that Mom created for herself. She had only been married to Dad for three years. She wasn't prepared for motherhood. The news devastated her. Her mother was a homemaker, and she had no intentions to do the same. But Dad convinced her that

God's timing was perfect timing, so she began to prepare for my birth.

After my birth, she experienced some pain from the surgical procedure in which I was delivered when the nurse placed me in her arms. "Have you chosen a name for her?"

"Yes. Her name is Jacqueline Classie Jones."

Jake Mercy

The morning *humidity* creates sweat on Mercy's masculine body. He woke up at five a.m. to run his routine two miles. The earlier the run, the easier it is for him to be motivated.

The peaceful scenery in the community of El Club Verde, where he resides, in Southlake, persuades him to run an extra mile. He's surrounded by green rolling hills, post oak trees, and beautiful ponds. But his peaceful run is disrupted by a thin blonde doubled over in pain.

His paramedic senses kick in. "Ma'am." He attempts to make eye contact with her. "Are you okay?"

"I'm having trouble breathing."

"Can you straighten up?"

She stands up straight.

Their eyes meet; his world stands still. Her eyes are bright and blue. Her lips are lovely.

He shakes off their attraction. "Sit down since you are experiencing dyspnea."

She sits on the bench.

He lowers his stance to meet her gaze. "I'll give you medical instructions to help. Rest your feet flat on the ground. Lean your chest slightly forward. Rest your elbows on your knees."

She follows his instructions.

He continues, "Now breathe in slowly through your nose. Keep your mouth closed. Don't take any deep breaths. Breathe a routine breath."

She slightly leans forward exposing her breasts.

"Hold up!" He looks away. "Your tank top is exposing your breasts."

She rushes to fix the issue. "I'm sorry. That was an accident." She attempts to stand but staggers.

"Whoa!" he says and grabs her arms to prevent her from falling.

She takes a few deep breaths. "I'm feeling better now. Thank you, Jake Mercy. I appreciate you being a Good Samaritan."

"You know who I am?"

She giggles like a schoolgirl. "Everyone knows who you are."

"Well, you look familiar to me, too. Do you have a name?" he asks, eyebrows raised.

She smiles with delight. "Chase Daniels."

"I didn't realize you lived in my neighborhood."

"I don't. My sister does. You do remember sleeping with her last night, don't you?"

"Brittany Daniels." He pauses. "Please tell me you're not going to publish that information in *Sporting It Magazine?"*

He cuts across his green manicured yard, and rests on the edge of a bronze angelic water fountain. He listens to the tranquil sound of the flowing water and allows it to relax his mind. But at the bottom of the fountain, copper pennies shine, shine like she used to.

He refuses to envision the accident that ended their relationship. He suppresses his tears. He looks up at the sun after feeling its burn on his shoulders. It's time for him to cool off.

He runs through his house. Pulls off his shirt. Opens the back door. Dives into the swimming pool. The chilly water gratifies his aching soul.

Flat on his back, he feels his toned muscles relax. But the formation of mental images from the accident invades his thoughts.

His wedding anniversary is approaching, and the torment of the divorce burns into his mind like a tattoo burns into skin.

When Mercy was a teenager, his grandfather told him that relationships were successful when built on simple things like God and kissing.

He did listen to his grandfather's advice. He purchased magazines from a bookstore to gather information, researched types of kisses, and how to perform them. On his second date with me, he put that knowledge into practice.

He waited in the foyer at Jones Ranch when I came down the stairs in a pair of yellow rain boots holding a picnic basket. I explained to him what made me happy. "Poles, bait, picnics, and rain boots is all I'll ever need to be content."

We fished from his truck's tailgate while he executed a plan to kiss me.

"Hey, Classie. Let's make a bet. The fisherman who catches the most fish will kiss the loser. The winner will choose the kiss. The loser will jump in the pond."

I considered the bet, but I was an expert, and could easily defeat him. However, I wanted to kiss Jake Mercy, the star football receiver at Tye High School, so I executed my plan to lose. "You have yourself a bet. But I have a question for you?"

"Ask."

"Earlier you said the winner of the bet can choose a kiss. How many types of kisses are there?"

"Numerous ones. Don't worry. I don't mind practicing them with you."

And he did, after he (won) the bet. "3 for me. 1 for you," he bragged. But before he finished his sentence, I jumped from the tailgate into the pond.

"Classie!" he yelled. "I didn't think you would jump. You're going to freeze in that chilly water." He ran to the truck and grabbed his brown coat from the front seat. I was lying on the bench inside the cabana when he returned.

My long, wavy brown hair was dripping wet. The water caused my coveralls to cling tight to my legs, and my yellow rain boots were muddy.

Mercy placed his coat around my shoulders. He waited until I stopped shivering to place his arm around my neck. "You're one crazy chick," he said, and focused on my big, brown eyes. "Your eyes sparkle like copper pennies." Butterflies took flight in Mercy's stomach. It was his first time to ever feel them. His chest felt odd. It became difficult for him to breathe. His hands were clammy. His heart was beating fast. He continued to stare into my eyes as his lips quivered. He leaned in and pressed his lips to my cheek.

"That's our first kiss?" I asked. I had to react quickly to salvage it. I positioned my hand behind his head and pulled him in. The kiss was sweet and simple. The warmness that I felt on my lips sent a shiver down my spine.

Mercy smiled after I released him.

"What type of kiss was that?" I asked.

"A practice one!" He slipped his tongue into my mouth.

After Mercy swims, he packs a suitcase and leaves for Tye Town. Upon his arrival, he reads a wooden (Mercy Mansion) rustic sign planted at the driveway of Mercy Ranch and then enters the secular passcode to the automatic gate.

An excitement flows through his body when he sees his mother's vehicle parked in the driveway. He grabs his bags and rushes towards the front door. But before he makes it inside, Lucy Mercy, his mother, embraces him. He picks her up and twirls her around in circles. She did the same to him when he was a small boy.

"Joseph Jake Mercy," she screams, "I've missed you!"

He gently releases her. "Mom, but you call me daily."

The outside oasis at Mercy Mansion is his favorite spot. The in-ground custom pool is surrounded by stones and patio. It features an eight-person built-in hot tub. The coolness of the water coming from the waterfall above the cabana splashes him in the face. He's sitting under it having lunch with his mother.

"I've prepared your favorite bologna with mustard and pepper sandwich," she says placing a plate in front of him.

"I haven't had one of these since Classie made me one." He pauses. "Did I tell you I saw her yesterday at the lake house?"

Lucy fills his glass with water. "Did you tell her?"

"No."

"Why didn't you tell her you're returning to football?"

"Sex got in our way," he replies with a laugh.

"You didn't?"

"I did. But she probably already knows about football. Her best friend, Gianna Perkins, is my sports agent's girlfriend."

Lucy gathers their plates. "Are we living in a small world, or did you already know that Classie's best friend is dating your new sports agent?"

He winks, and asks, "Is Earl staying here tonight? Because I can find a hotel in town if I need to."

"Earl will not be staying here this weekend. You're welcome to stay with me."

"Then I'll stay here tonight, but the rest of the weekend I plan on staying at the house that I once shared with Classie." He hesitates. "I sold it."

Lucy drops the plates, shattering glass. "I thought you planned on keeping it. Have you lost hope in reconciliation?"

He bends over and gathers up the broken pieces of glass. "Like this glass, we will forever be broken."

She glances at him with disappointment. "Then why did you have sex with her?"

Supernatural

It's morning and he's ready to run. The first mile he runs comes easy for him. The second mile is a bit harder. One more mile to go uphill and he will reach his destination to Jones Ranch to tell me he's returning to football.

But a white sports car traveling at a high rate of speed heads towards him. He jumps out of the way to prevent from being struck and lands in tall grass.

His legs are scratched from the fall. Dirt covers his body. He brushes the dirt off, and then notices the car has crashed into a tree.

He runs over to the accident scene. A female with golden blonde hair is trapped inside. Her head is against the steering wheel. He tries to open the driver's door, but it's jammed. He runs to the passenger side, and it won't open either.

At a full sprint he runs until he reaches the entrance to Jones Ranch where my red pickup is parked at the entrance.

He waves his hands in the air to grab my attention.

From a distance, I roll down the window.

He yells, "Classie, there's been an automobile accident a mile up the road. Call 9-1-1!" Without any further instructions he runs back to the scene.

I call 9-1-1 to report the accident. After I place the call, I drive to the scene. "Do you need help?" I ask, my voice shivers.

But he's pre-occupied. He isn't paying attention to me. I watch him struggle with the doors which appear to be jammed, so I locate a window breaker from my truck and take it to him.

He runs over to the passenger side and breaks the window out. He crawls through the window, across the seat, and reaches the driver. He gently raises the injured female's head from the steering wheel. He notices a severe abrasion to her forehead. He kicks the driver's side door until it pops open.

He exits the car and removes the woman from the wreckage. He places her gently on the ground and checks for a pulse. She's breathing. He rips off his shirt and applies pressure to a severe wound on her forehead. From a distance a siren sounds.

I'm watching him work, and I'm impressed with his physical body. I slowly walk over to the woman and notice that her hair is bloody. Her skin is clammy. Her thin lips are pale. Her eyes are closed.

Mercy looks up at me. "She looks pretty bad," he softly whispers.

"She looks as bad as you looked on the day of our accident," I reply.

"Her pulse and breathing are rapid. She's going into shock," he declares. "Will you help her?"

I consider helping her, but opt out, as fear washes over me.

"Then do you have something in your truck that I can cover her with?"

"I have a blanket."

He rips off the woman's shirt to check for chest injuries.

"Here," I say and hand the blanket to him.

"She's losing too much blood," he says, as he focuses on the injury to her forehead.

I suspect he has a relationship with this woman, as compassion for them rushes in like a flood, so I intervene and run my hand over the deep wound on her forehead.

The wound closes.

He elevates her feet and places the blanket over her body.

The ambulance arrives.

"Do you know her?"

He nods. "I'm riding with her to the hospital," he replies and steps inside the ambulance.

The Sacrifice

I return to Jones Ranch exhausted after a cross country run. I haven't talked to my parents since my arrival, but I've been invited to a party hosted by my mother this evening.

I remove a sweaty tank top and gym shorts, and step inside a tan tiled shower. A typical hot shower is not in the cards for me today. I must have a cold one to revive myself. I inhale my lemon aroma body wash to awaken my senses, and rush to wash my hair with my mother's awful smelling shampoo. *It's tea tree, I think.*

I quickly remove a white, fluffy, nice smelling towel from the white vanity cabinet in my bathroom, and then glide across the bedroom to the huge walk-in closet where I pull a satin yellow mid-length dress from its hanger.

I dry my hair and allow my natural curls to dangle down. I apply brown mascara, red lipstick, and a bronzer to my face.

I remove a two-piece yellow swimsuit from the dresser to use as undergarments and cover up with the satin dress. I complete my classy style with a pair of silver ankle strap high heels.

The handrails on the stairs are oily, but I use them as an anchor to prevent me from falling in heels. "These handrails have too much furniture oil on them. We need to wipe them down," I say to Norma as she runs to answer the doorbell.

"Hey," she says with a punch to Mercy's arm. "We didn't know if you'd be able to make it."

My eyes journey to his profile. His blonde hair is shaved. His baby blue eyes are bright. His full lips are quivering. He's nervous; I see it in his demeanor. The blue t-shirt he's wearing clings to his broad shoulders. His cowboy jeans are starched, and his cowboy boots are polished. He's dressed to impress. But who is he dressed to impress?

"Did you bring a date?" Norma asks after she notices my attraction towards him.

He nods and his date walks in behind him.

Her tousled hair is edgy, and her tight ruffled dress flatters her curvy figure. I can't deny that she's beautiful, but the fact he has brought a date to my house makes me madder than a hornet.

I take a step forward to clear the last stair, but my high heel catches the edge of it, and I fall forwards.

He reacts quickly and slides his arms under my body to prevent my fall. He cradles me in his arms. And just like that— I draw him in.

His date clears her throat.

We exchange a quick glance before he helps me stand.

"Did I miss something?" my father asks, as he joins us in the foyer.

I adjust the strap on my heel. "It seems Mercy's quick actions have saved two women today. I tripped and almost broke my neck, and his date had a car crash and almost lost her life. But it appears she's better now."

She touches the bandage on her forehead. "It's only a scratch."

"Only a scratch," I say with a slight laugh.

"And my name is Chase Daniels."

"I know who you are. Your father is the former general manager for the Dallas Wardens, and you're a reporter for *Sporting It Magazine."*

She nods and takes Mercy's hand. "And I was a former Dallas Wranglers cheerleader."

I snicker under my breath. "And I thought you were flawless."

"Not a fan?" she asks.

Mercy snickers. "Classie likes Washington. There's something about burgundy that turns her on."

Dad senses our undeniable chemistry. "Your mother invited several guests to this party. If you'd like to join her in the backyard, I'm sure she could use a hand."

"I'll lend her a hand."

A rectangular pool, a built-in hot tub, and an outside kitchen highlights our backyard. Ten white lounge chairs, two separate white tables, with six sets of chairs, surround the pool.

"Welcome home. I'm sorry I missed your arrival," Mom says with an embrace. "Why is John huddled in the foyer with Jake?"

"The question should be why did Mercy bring a date?"

Mom takes me by the upper arm and whispers, "For goodness sakes Classie, y'all are divorced."

My temper peeks. "I never wanted to sign those divorce papers. Don't you ever forget that!"

"Attention everyone. I'd like to introduce you to my newest client and the reason that I've thrown this little get together this evening. I'm honored that Colt Karr, the quarterback for the Dallas Wranglers, has allowed me to help him out," Mom says with a smile.

Like Brett Rainey, Colt's been featured on the cover of *Sporting It Magazine,* and tonight, he's fashionably dressed in a slim gray suit, red shirt, and gray tie. He's tall, dark, and handsome, and better looking in person than on a cover of a magazine.

Mom continues, "It has been my pleasure finding him real estate located right here in Tye Town. So, y'all please welcome him to our neighborhood." Mom pats him on the back. I watch Mercy shuffle through the crowd and stand near her. "And we are celebrating Jake Mercy's return to football."

I glance at Mercy with pained eyes; he didn't tell me about the news at the lake house.

"Thanks everyone. I appreciate y'all coming. It means a lot to me. This is a dream come true," Mercy says.

The following morning, I wake up and slip on my coveralls and rain boots. My plan is to release my anger towards Mercy by fishing.

I grab my fishing gear from the garage and start up my recreational vehicle.

Honk.

Honk.

It's Mercy.

"Go home! I don't have the strength to face you today," I say and ride in the direction of the pond.

He jumps on another recreational vehicle and follows me.

The flowers are in bloom, the insects are circling, and the frogs are leaping from lily pad to lily pad at the pond.

"The Texas Dawn lilies are in full bloom, flamboyant yellow just like the dress you wore last night," he says.

I huff under my breath. "I'm surprised you even noticed me!"

He shifts uncomfortably on the vehicle. "Are you going to have a negative attitude with me today like you did last night?"

"What kind of attitude would you like for me to have?" I slide my leg over to dismount from the vehicle.

He dismounts from his vehicle, too. "What do you want from me?"

A hint of rage reaches my lips. "An apology!"

"For what?"

"For divorcing me and not telling me you're returning to football!"

He closes his eyes and takes a deep breath. "I was paralyzed when I divorced you." He shifts towards me. "Haven't we gone over this? I couldn't imagine you having to take care of me for the rest of your life."

I gesture towards his strong legs. "But I did take care of you." I pause. "It took a year after the accident, but your legs eventually healed."

He stares at me, unsure if he should address the truth. "My dreams are coming true because you healed them." He moves in closer and runs his hands along the sides of my arms. "We haven't talked about my healing in over a year. Why did you move to San Antonio without an explanation?"

"I had to get away from Tye to accept what had happened to me. The bridge's collapse changed everything for me. My near-death experience had given me a gift that I'm still afraid to use."

"That's why you hesitated to help Chase?" He takes a step back. "I planned on telling you about my return to football at the lake house. And I know that I promised you that I wouldn't play again, but I miss playing. It's been three years since our accident. It's been two years since you healed me. I've been a paramedic for a year, but it's not what I'm passionate about. I need to play football."

"Regardless of the outcome?"

"I know what you've said you've dreamed. But I can't allow your dreams to rob me of my destiny."

I sigh. "The choice is yours to make." I walk toward him, staring at his lips. His eyes burn into me. I tiptoe to kiss him.

After we stop kissing, I say, "I will not save you again."

After an emotional day at the pond, I climb into bed, and once more, I recall the accident.

The wooden bridge had collapsed. Powerful winds launched Mercy into the air. He landed at the bottom of the creek with the recreational vehicle on top of his legs. And I landed on the edge of the creek bank near a big tree.

But suddenly, a transparent image appeared before me. "Give up, and give in to me," a powerful voice commanded.

I identified the image as Death.

I struggled to stand and was having a tough time breathing. Everything that I lived through, during my life, flashed before my eyes.

A white light guided me through a white tunnel, and then placed me in a field of green pasture where I rested.

I was surrounded by a clear pond when the white light disappeared, and a Samson-like strength overcame me.

My mind was at peace until I felt an uncontrollable pain in my stomach. I leaned over and vomit viciously hurled into the creek. I was wishing that I was back in greener pastures. I cried out to God, "Today I've defeated Death. Today, God, you gave me mercy! But Mercy, where was he?" He was thrown from his recreational vehicle the last time I saw him.

Minutes later, I made it to his lifeless body which was fully immersed in the water. I waded into the creek and pushed the vehicle off his legs. But he wasn't breathing. In one motion, I swooped him up.

But when I laid him down, I felt a river of blood gushing out from underneath my insides. The sight of blood made me a bit queasy. Ignoring the pain in my stomach, I checked his injuries. There was an abrasion by his ear. I removed my tank top and applied pressure to his wound. "You never listen to me. You're stubborn as a mule. I told you it wasn't safe to cross the bridge."

Repositioning his body, I placed my hands in the center of his chest between his nipples and pressed down. I counted to thirty.

Lowering my mouth to his, I gave him two breaths. I repeated the life-saving procedure three times. On the third time, he began to breathe.

I prayed for him before I whispered, "I will always love you."

I rested my head on his chest and closed my eyes. "God, if he goes, I go," I declared. In that moment I remembered a beach bag that I left at the boat dock. My cellular phone was inside of it.

I noticed the storm had passed, so I glanced at the creek. The water roared and rushed over the rocks. But I knew I'd have to wade into the creek again to call for help.

"Classie," I heard him whisper, "I can't feel my legs."

"But you're alive," I replied as I shed tears. "I need to go call for help."

"If you go get help, don't come back for me. Leave me here to die. If I can't play football, then I don't want to live," he said.

I considered my options. If I moved again, I would miscarry our child. I hesitated but waded into the creek. Mercy's life depended on me and saving him was my only option.

The beach bag was under an iron table on the boat dock when I found it. I held up the phone. No signal. I carried it towards the creek until I received one.

"Collin County 9-1-1. What is your emergency?" the dispatcher asked.

"My name is Classie Jones Mercy. I've been in an accident, with my husband, at my family's lake. My husband is severely injured, and I think I've miscarried our child. Please send us an ambulance." I looked up at the heavens as the clouds gave way and the sun came out. I continued, "The address is…"

The Enemy

Forcing myself to recall the accident last night made me realize how blessed I am to be alive this morning. I greet my family in a white sheer tank top, light blue overalls, and flip flops, "Good morning."

"Someone is in a good mood," Mom replies.

"It's the day before the Fourth of July. And I've been invited by Gianna to the social event of the year."

"I heard Senator Perkins was having his annual charity fundraiser in Dallas. Shall I take you shopping for a dress?" Mom asks and sips her coffee.

I consider her offer. Although my mother and I aren't very close, she was the woman who taught me about fashion and how to catch a man.

It was my sophomore year in high school, when Mom said, "You must use attitude, clothes, makeup, and shoes to lure them in."

She escorted me to shoe stores, vintage stores, and department stores. She introduced me to the styles of her two favorite fashion influences Jacqueline Kennedy Onassis and Marilyn Monroe.

The first store we visited was a shoe store where we spent hours. My mother said, "Marilyn Monroe made high-heels chic. If you want to be a lending light in fashion, Marilyn's style is a beneficial place to begin. High heels can help make a woman feel confident. They're fashion sense number one."

She showed me a kitten heel. "Choose the color of your high heel. This is a starter high heel. It will give you a tiny bit of extra height. You'll wear them out of the store."

I chose a black pair, but my favorite heels were the ankle strap heels.

The second store we visited was a vintage store with classic dresses. "Classie, take some advice from your mother. If you want class, never show your ass. Dresses are fashion sense number two."

She escorted me around the store, showing off a wrap, a mini, a sheath, a slip, a baby doll, an empire, a shift, a maxi, and a suit dress. "Choose a maxi dress. They have fun prints."

When we finished shopping for a dress and shoes, I visited a department store for proper makeup application. Mom said to the makeup clerk, "Makeup is fashion sense number three."

As a natural beauty, I wasn't a fan of makeup. However, I did fall in love with red lipstick.

On the drive home from shopping, Mom explained to me that a woman's attitude is what matters most. "Be confident. Be polite. Be exceptional. Express yourself in a respectable manner, and you'll attract respectable men. Jacqueline Kennedy was the finest example of this."

And she was right. After I met Mercy, my style, attitude, and physical appearance all changed. I began to step towards womanhood. I challenged myself to compete harder in track. My workouts became more intense. My entire body toned up. I was a top ranked track athlete and won a state high school championship.

After Mom and I shopped for my social event of the year dress, I throw myself into hair and makeup. Then, I call Gianna to check to see if she's ready. She tells me that Brett Rainey has been asking about me and apologizes for leaving me alone with Mercy at the lake house.

"It's okay. Mercy has a strange way of getting what he wants from me."

I valet park at *Hotel Amore* in Dallas. Gianna is the first person I meet in the lobby. She looks her best in a form fitting, wrap, green ruffle dress, with criss cross lace exposing her sexy back. Her long, red hair is neither plain nor boring. It's beautifully pinned up on top of her head, and her perfectly applied eyeshadow makes her green eyes stand out. "My father should be arriving any minute now, and I can't wait for you to meet him."

"Is there a restroom where I can tidy up?"

She gestures towards the elevator. "Second floor. First door on the left."

I locate the restroom after shuffling through wall-to-wall people. I need to approve my look before I meet Senator Perkins.

I stare into the mirror and acknowledge my mother has some fashion sense. I look like a fairy tale princess in a gold, sleeve, floor length dress. The bodice is accented with beads. And since I was blessed with natural waves, I allowed my tresses down. And if that's not lust worthy, I created perfect makeup with liquid bronzer, bronze blush, and bronze eyeshadow. I take in a breath and exit the restroom.

"I'm impressed with your beauty," a strange man says, leaned up against the wall near the restroom. He smiles with adorable dimples. His swooning eyes seducing me.

"I'm spellbound."

He comes closer and lifts my chin with one finger. As I gaze into his green eyes, a vision of my battle with death invades my thoughts. I look away to break the spell. "What is the name of the man that is trying to take control of my thoughts?"

"My name is Cullen Cash."

I heavily sigh. "I sense your dislike for me."

"I don't dislike you, Miss Jones. I respect you." He's suppressing the urge to touch me. "I want you to be part of my team. I'm here to encourage you to use your gifts."

I grin at him. "I don't know what gifts you're referring to."

He places his hands on both sides of my face. "You were born to serve mankind." His mouth near mine. "Shall I list your gifts?"

I softly place my hands on top of his, as he continues to look into my eyes.

"You hear voices that most humans aren't able to hear. You see things that most humans can't see. You detect odors that most humans can't smell. You heal with the touch of your hand." He moves his hands from my face.

"I haven't experienced some of those gifts."

"But you will. You're a protector. And you'll do whatever it takes to rescue others. In fact, I'm banking on that!"

It isn't easy to walk away from him, but somehow, I manage.

Inside the elevator, I take a deep breath. Am I ready to see Rainey again? After that weird encounter- I am.

"You look gorgeous," Matt says greeting me at the entrance of the ballroom.

"You don't look too shabby yourself. Has Senator Perkins arrived yet?"

He gestures towards the stage. "He's the gentleman on the platform."

I take a step forward, but then I back track. "Matt, do you know a man named Cullen Cash?"

He nods. "He's the head of security for the Texas Royal Sports Family. Jasper James is in attendance tonight."

"But Senator Perkins is a Republican. Isn't the Texas Royal Sports Family Democrats?"

"No. I believe Marilyn Maverick James is the only Democrat in the family."

I try to smile, still engulfed by the eyes of Cullen Cash, before I approach Gianna's father. "Senator Perkins," I say, a bit loud, "I'm Classie Jones!"

"It's about time we meet." He steps off the platform. "Gianna has told me so much about the dispatcher that became her best friend."

"Well Senator, Gianna is the bravest police officer I know, even though you don't agree with her occupation."

"Police officers are brave. I have no beef with her occupation. My only beef is that she chose not to become a doctor." He shifts towards me. "I hope you enjoy the party."

"Thank you for the invitation."

"Have you been sitting by yourself long?"

"Rainey," I say, and greet him with a smile. I gaze at his sexy style in a luxury black tuxedo and green tie. "I'd be honored if you'd keep me company?"

"Well, you don't have to ask me twice," he says, as his hand gently brushes over mine.

He sits, as my gaze strays to Senator Perkins talking to Cullen Cash.

"I've known Gianna's father since I was a small boy. He's extremely hard on her."

My eyes return to Rainey. "You're childhood friends with Gianna? I thought you knew her through Matt."

"That's what I like about Gianna. She's never abused our friendship. Most women brag about having famous friends. But not her. And I'm the one who set her up with Matt. I thought they'd make the perfect couple."

I raise an eyebrow and gesture towards an exotic woman sitting near the platform. "That woman over there is looking at you like you're a piece of meat."

"That woman is Gianna's mother. She's a former Miss Texas."

"And apparently, she's a cougar," I say with a laugh. "Maybe that's why Gianna doesn't like to discuss her parent's relationship with me. I'm even surprised she allowed Senator Perkins to invite me."

Rainey's sultry eyes gaze at my lips. "I was the one who asked Senator Perkins to invite you."

"Why?" I am surprised.

"I wanted to see you again."

"But I left you standing alone at a bar."

"You left me mesmerized."

I try to listen to his heartfelt confession, but Gianna's mother continues to stare at us. "She has a thing for you, doesn't she?"

His lips part. "At one time, yes. But please stop looking at her. I'd rather you look at me the way she does."

And for a solid moment, I do. But my curiosity kills the cat, and I quickly look at her again.

"Shall we go meet the cougar?" he asks taking my hand.

"**Brett**," she says with a sexy tone, "It's a joy to see you."

She addresses him by his first name.

"Likewise, **Mrs.Perkins**," he says, putting an emphasis on the salutation, "I thought you'd like to meet my date since you've been staring her down. This is Classie Jones, Gianna's best friend."

She's quick to greet me with a hug. "Gianna raves about you. And she's correct. Miss Jones, you're gorgeous." She looks at my shoes. "Where did you buy your heels?"

"My mother actually picked these out for me."

"Well, she has excellent taste." She places her hand on Rainey's back and slowly rubs it. "I hope you and Classie have a marvelous time."

"I'm certain we will."

"Jake Mercy. Come meet Senator Perkins!" Matt's voice rings out across the ballroom.

We shift our attention to the platform where Mercy is sporting a polished, slim fit, blue suit, and Chase, a blue, floral lace, tulle dress.

"Do you know him?" Carol asks, after she observes me looking at Mercy likes he's a piece of meat.

"I was married to him."

"That surprises me."

"And why is that?"

She devours his profile with vulture eyes. "He likes to sleep around. And I was under the impression, Miss Jones, that you're a woman with Christian morals."

"He hasn't always been a player, **Mrs**. Perkins." I put an emphasis on the Mrs. "In fact, Mercy and I waited to have sex after we wed."

Rainey observes Mercy biting his lip, as Mercy stares at me. "It appears he may still be in love with you."

"At one time, yes. But please stop looking at him. I'd rather you look at me like he does."

Rainey shifts closer.

"He already does, Miss Jones," Carol replies observing Rainey's mesmerized gaze.

Rainey grasps my hand. "Shall we get this party started?"

I give him a polite smile and allow him to lead me to the dance floor.

He pulls me in close. "Wanna learn how to play baseball?" he asks with a wink.

"I'm more of a football fan," I reply with a laugh.

He looks at me with interest. "You've got to make it to first base. But I must warn you that it's hard to hit off me. I'm the best pitcher in baseball."

"Then I'll try not to strike out." My eyes cut towards Jasper James; he's sitting at the Perkins' table. "How relevant is Jasper James?"

"He replaced Jason Daniels this season. He's the youngest general manager in baseball history at the age of twenty-six."

"He's my age?"

He nods, and then grinds against my thigh. "I'm sure you read about my scandal with his sister, Jocelyn Maverick James?"

"I moved to San Antonio last fall when all that was going on. I've heard some rumors. Would you like to discuss her?"

"I'd rather we not talk about her. I've let the past stay in the past."

The music ends.

Rainey leads me off the dance floor.

"I'll be back. I need to use the restroom," I say and exit the ballroom.

Mercy follows me out. "Did you have fun dancing with Brett Rainey?" he asks with a smirk.

I have an eerie feeling we're being watched. My feeling is accurate. "Cullen Cash. Do you like ease dropping?" I ask, as he mysteriously interferes.

"It's surprising to me that Rainey would be interested in a woman like you," he interjects. "He's the most popular pitcher in baseball. He's been featured on multiple magazine covers, and I think he deserves a woman who shares the same social status."

"A woman like Jocelyn James?"

"Jocelyn Maverick James," he sternly corrects. He gazes down at me. "She's perfect for him."

"There you are," Rainey says, as he joins us near the elevator. He looks at Cullen, and then frowns at my expression. "Did I miss something?"

"Yes. You did." I shift towards Rainey. "Mr. Cash was telling me that I don't deserve to be with you."

"Is that true?" Rainey asks.

Cullen studies me. "That's not entirely true. I said you need a woman that shares the same social status."

I look at Mercy. "And do you believe Jake Mercy needs a woman with the same social status?" I ask Cullen in anger.

Cullen smirks. "I believe he's found one."

"I know I don't have a celebrity status like them, but I used to be a star athlete in high school."

"Used to be," Cullen replies sarcastically.

My face heats under his smirk. "I turned a track and field scholarship down because I was married to Mercy and wanted to see him fulfill his dreams!"

"And how did that turn out for you?" Cullen looks at my belly.

Rainey leans in and whispers, "How about we get out of here? I'll leave my contribution to the Perkins Foundation at the front desk."

The First Date

It's my first date with Rainey. I light the candles on the iron table, at our lake's boat dock, to help keep the bugs at bay. "Don't you have family you'd rather celebrate the Fourth of July with?" I ask him before laying on a lounge chair in a red bikini.

He extends his body out in the lounger next to me. "My family is at *Warden Park* watching the game."

"And why didn't you have to attend the game?"

"My shoulder injury is considered severe. I was placed on 60-day injured reserved, which is why I'm not required to attend the games or stay with the team."

I frown as I position the lounger upwards. "Which is why you were in San Antonio?"

"Yes. There's a surgeon there that evaluated my injury. I'll be having surgery the day after tomorrow," he replies, his brown eyes consuming my insecurities.

I grab a swimsuit cover up.
"I've always detested my small breasts."

"You're a beautiful woman. You should be proud of your body." He leans forward and murmurs, "I think they're perfect." His gaze raises to my lips. "Like your lips."

I reciprocate his forwardness and lean in.

His mouth finds mine.

After his pleasuring kiss, he asks, "How did you like making it to first base?"

"It was too easy. I thought you said you were the best pitcher in baseball?"

His laugh is contagious. "Shall we take a dip in the lake?"

I watch him move off the lounger. Nice upper arms. Six pack abdominals. And strong legs. He runs and jumps off the boat dock.

I remove my cover up, place it on the lounger, and follow suit.

He swims over to me. His hands move beneath me to steady us. He runs his tongue along my lower lip and then slips it inside my mouth.

After our swim, I assemble a cane-pole and attach the line, bobber, and hook.

Rainey looks impressed. "Shall I bait your hook?"

"You watched me rig the pole. I assure you I can bait a hook, too." I grab the coffee can and retrieve a minnow. Then, I hand him a pole.

I cast.

He casts.

I reel.

He reels.

After an hour lapses, I look at my phone. "Time is up. How many fish did you catch?"

"2," he replies with a smile.

I tell him about my past fishing bets with Mercy.

He whispers, "Since this is our first fishing adventure together, you'll have to settle for a forehead kiss." He gently kisses my forehead.

I swallow hard. "What if I told you I want a seductive kiss?"

He points at the lounger. "Lay on your stomach." He reaches inside an ice chest and places a piece of ice in his mouth. Sitting on his knees, he positions the ice on the small of my back. The cold causes me to flinch. He moves the ice with his tongue from one side of my back to the other side, and then presses his lips into my skin. When he reaches my shoulder blades in a commanding sexy voice he says, "Roll over!"

I respect his command and roll over.

He forces the ice inside my mouth with his tongue and leaves me longing for more.

Rainey flew to San Antonio this morning; I had no idea that he could kiss me as well as Mercy, and perhaps even better. To distract me from thinking about him, I join Norma at the pool.

"When did you start wearing a two-piece bikini? And how did you manage to hide that tattoo on your side from our dad?" Norma asks, as I wade into the pool.

"Gianna and I were inked this spring. And I think I look rather cute in this bikini. What would you say if I told you I wanted to get breast implants?"

"I would say that you have lost your mind."

I gaze at my breasts, and reply, "It's rumored that Mercy slept with Jenny. Do you think it was because she had large breasts?"

Norma rolls her eyes. "The elegant Jacqueline Classie Jones has transitioned from a woman who acted like Jacqueline Kennedy to a woman who is acting like Marilyn Monroe. And our father thinks I'm the wild one." She shuffles out of the pool and grabs a towel from the cabana. "And Jake didn't sleep with her because of her breasts; he slept with her because he wasn't himself."

"So, the rumor is true? He slept with her last fall after I moved."

"It's true. But you should hear the truth from him. He watched fireworks with us last night. I think he was hoping you'd join us."

"We married on July 4th. I needed to avoid the memory." I wade out of the pool and grab my cover up from a lounger. "And I spent the 4th with Rainey at the lake. Believe this. We created our own fireworks."

I follow Norma to the guest house. "When are you and Tony moving out of this place? Aren't you ready for your own home?"

"No. I like living with my parents," she replies with a smile.

We head to the kitchen for drinks. "I think I really like Rainey. We had an enjoyable time last night. And when he kissed me, I wanted to fornicate with him. But waiting for marriage is important to me." I open the refrigerator and grab a bottled water. "Or it was." I pause. "I kind of fornicated with Mercy at the lake house."

"You what?"

"It was a mistake. It'll never happen again."

"Then you should have sex with Brett Rainey. But do not tell Dad I said that. He would kill me. And try to forget about Jake Mercy."

Buzz. The doorbell rings.

Norma rushes to answer it. "Speaking of the devil," she says returning with Mercy.

He appears at the kitchen doorway in blue swim shorts, a fitted t-shirt, and flip flops. "Hello."

"What do you want?"

He leans against the doorway's frame. "Can we talk?" he asks, and winks at Norma.

"Yes. Meet me by the pool," I say and toss the bottled water into the trash can.

"Good luck," Norma whispers.

He conceals his smile. "You look good in a two-piece swimsuit. You should wear one more often."

"Why are you here?" I ask, perturbed.

He removes his t-shirt and throws it like a football onto the lounger. I watch him walk to the diving board and dive in. After he resurfaces, he floats in silence.

"Why are you here?"

He leans against the wall of the pool. "To tell you that I've sold our house to Colt Karr."

I stop breathing for a moment. "That's why my mother had the party the other night. That's what she was trying to tell me, but I was too consumed watching you flirt with Chase."

"It was a difficult decision, but I purchased a home in Southlake last year, and since you live in San Antonio, I felt like it was the right thing to do."

"For you!" My voice is loud. "You've always been selfish, but even for you this is too much. You're so inconsiderate. What about the stuff in the nursery?"

He wades out of the pool like a tyrant. His eyes are pained. "I will never forgive you for saving my life and allowing our child to die. And if you want the stuff in the nursery, then I suggest you go get it!" Like a deadly tornado, he storms towards the cabana and grabs a chair. He tosses it into the pool. And then another one.

"Enough!" I shout, as I wait for him to calm down. "That's why you divorced me, wasn't it? It wasn't because you were paralyzed. It was because I miscarried our child."

His eyes acknowledge the truth. "Meet me at our house in an hour."

Moving On

I decide to grab a suitcase and stay overnight at our house before Colt Karr moves in. I place my luggage on the living room couch, and then I walk into the kitchen and open every kitchen cabinet in search for pain medication.

I grab a bottle of over-the-counter medication but toss it into the trash can. It's not potent enough to achieve the relief I need from Mercy's honest confession. *He blames me for our child's death.*

I notice a prescription medication prescribed to him; it's Vicodin, so I take one. I take in a deep breath before moving on to my next vice, a bottle of wine in the refrigerator. I grab it and walk to the nursery where a white crib has a yellow cotton comforter placed snugly inside it.

Hours later, Mercy finds me passed out on the floor with the empty bottle of wine next to me. He tries to revive me. "Classie," he whispers. But I am unconscious, *not dead.*

He cradles me in his arms and carries me upstairs to the master bedroom where he undresses me and tucks me in. He kisses my forehead and then goes downstairs where he locates the Vicodin and disposes of it in the garbage disposal.

He looks at the clock on his phone and notices it's nine p.m. He removes his t-shirt and shoes and rests on the couch.

His phone's alarm startles him. It's five a.m., but his two-mile run will have to wait.

He prepares a scrambled egg breakfast for me. He freshly squeezes orange juice and pours it in a tall transparent glass. He places my breakfast on a white serving tray and returns upstairs to me.

He places the tray on the bedroom's dresser. "Wake up!"

I roll over and stretch. "What happened to me? I feel like I've been in a train wreck."

He retrieves the tray from the dresser and places it in my lap. "You need to eat something. You'll need your strength today."

I fork the eggs. "Why?"

"We need to pack up the nursery."

I drink the orange juice. "Where am I supposed to take the stuff? I live in San Antonio in a tiny apartment. I have no room for it."

"You can afford a bigger one." He retrieves the tray from my lap. "Meet me in the nursery."

I slowly slip out of bed. "Wait!"

He stops and looks at me.

"Why am I wearing a Dallas Wranglers shirt?"

He laughs under his breath. "Because you had vomit on your shirt."

"And this is the only shirt you could find?"

He briefly smiles. "I know you're a Washington fan, but the Dallas Wranglers are always in style. If you'd like to change, then I put your luggage inside the closet."

He's packing baby clothes in a large box when I greet him in the nursery. "Thanks for breakfast."

"Not a problem."

I grab some baby clothes from the dresser drawer and help him finish packing. "I'd really like to find storage for these clothes."

"Why?" he asks and tapes the box shut.

"What happens if I find out I'm pregnant one day? I could use these."

He slightly frowns. He retrieves the boxes, and I follow him outside to his truck. "Classie, the doctor said that you'd never be able to have children. I don't understand why you're tormenting yourself like this." He places the boxes inside the truck. "But I'll store these in the attic at my house in Southlake. If you ever need them, you'll know where they'll be."

"Thank you," I say and quickly kiss him on the cheek. "Now, let me go get my luggage so you can lock up the house."

We return to the master bedroom. "When are you planning on moving the rest of your stuff out of the house?" I ask and stare at a photo on the dresser. "And why do you still have a picture of us on our wedding day?"

He ignores the question. "I've hired a moving company to pack up the rest." He gazes at my luggage. "Are you ready to go?"

I nod and reach for the luggage.

"No!" he says. "A woman should never carry her own luggage."

He places the luggage in the back of my truck. "I have a lunch date with my mother at *On a Dime Diner*. Would you like to join us?"

Though I am not sure it is a good idea, I agree.

***On a Dime Diner* is busy.** It's Mercy's favorite place to eat in Collin County.

When the waitress approaches, I lower my gaze at her belly. "How far are you?"

"Seven months."

"If you don't mind me asking, how old are you?"

"I'm eighteen. I got pregnant my senior year. Now, can I take your orders?"

Mercy orders a cheeseburger and a soda. I order a salad and a water.

"Did that bother you?" he asks as he watches the waitress waddle away.

"No. What bothers me is that you blamed me for the miscarriage!"

He avoids my gaze.

"And when are you going to stop sleeping with every woman you meet to fill a void?"

He reaches across the table, takes my chin, and tilts it upward. "Are you jealous?"

I slap his hand. "Why would I be jealous? I had you at the lake house. Or have you forgotten that?"

"Do you remember our wedding day?" he asks as the waitress places food in front of him. "I was nervous standing with your father at the altar."

"And I was nervous walking down the aisle with my mother praying that I didn't trip and fall in my heels." I fixate my eyes on him. "When I reached the altar, I noticed that you had tears in your eyes. You muttered the words I love you before taking my hand. A girl never forgets a sincere moment like that one."

He closes his eyes. "'Above all, love each other deeply, because love covers a multitude of sins.' John recited that during the ceremony."

I change the subject to suppress the memory. "How is Chase?" I fork my salad.

"She's good."

"And what about Jenny, have you seen her lately?"

He stops eating. "We were having an enjoyable conversation. Why did you have to ruin it?"

I huff. "I heard the rumors."

"Don't go there!" His voice loud.

I scan the café and look at all the inquiring eyes watching us.

He tosses money on the table to pay for the meal as his text tone goes off. "Mom had to cancel. Something came up with her boyfriend, Earl."

"I want to know what happened between you and Jenny."

"We were divorced. I don't owe you an explanation." He stands, leans forward, and kisses my forehead. "I really need to split. I have a date with Chase and her family at Lake Texoma tomorrow. Have a safe flight back to San Antonio. And tell Rainey I hope his surgery went well."

I can't help but wonder if he still loves me. "Was I another notch in your belt? Did the lake house mean nothing to you?"

He retraces his steps.

I lower my voice. "I'm sorry that you don't love me anymore."

"I loved you from day one. From the moment I saw you in high school, to the moment I married you, to the moment I divorced you, and yes, to the moment I made love to you at the lake house. There's never been a moment that I haven't loved you. But the moment you chose me over our child was the moment I lost respect for you."

Nestled on twelve private acres in a luxury community in San Antonio is Rainey's rental estate. He's staying here while he recovers from shoulder surgery.

Upon entry into the living room are two hand sculpted fireplaces. The walls are all hand plastered. There's a huge stained-glass window to provide natural light. "This place is amazing," I say and sit on a luxurious white leather couch with blue throw pillows.

"Thanks for coming. I didn't know if you'd have time to stop by since you just arrived back in town."

I look at his arm in a sling. "How's the shoulder?"

"Doc says I can start rehab in a few months. But I won't be able to return to baseball this season."

"Can you hold up your arm without the sling?"

He removes the sling and holds it up. "It feels like it's made of lead."

I sense his pain. "I know this will sound weird to you, but I think I can help with your progression. Will you sit on the floor in front of me?"

He sits on the floor.

Softly I rub my hand over his shoulder.

He releases a moan. "Wow. That feels good."

"And tomorrow you'll be better. And you'll return to baseball quicker than what they expected you to."

Ringtone. We start searching for our phones.

"I think it's yours," he says.

"Hello?"

"Classie. It's Lucy. Jake has been in a boating accident."

The Proposal

Red and blue lights flash when I run through the doubled doors of the emergency room.

"How did you get here so fast?" Lucy asks when I see her.

"Rainey has a helipad, and his pilot flew me here. How's Mercy?"

She shakes her head. "Not good. He was on the lake with Chase when their boat collided with another boat. He was underwater for over twenty minutes."

"But he was resuscitated?"

"Yes. But he's unresponsive."

"And Chase?"

She embraces me. "She's dead."

"I don't know what it is with you and water, but this has to stop," I say to Mercy and take a hold of his hand. "And I promised myself that I wouldn't save you again."

Lucy quietly enters the hospital room. "They're allowing both of us to visit him."

"I'll never understand why Mercy chose to marry me when he could have married any girl in high school."

"Because he said he would rather be with a girl who is kind and polite, can bait a hook, than a girl who is rude, arrogant, and full of herself."

"Then why did he sleep with Jenny last fall, and why did he choose to date a woman like Chase?"

Lucy reaches across the bed and touches my hand. "To this very day, I remember an impressive speech that you made in the fifth grade. May I recite it for you?"

I nod.

"Hi, my name is Jacqueline Classie Jones. My speech is about an elegant and stylish woman who my mother named me after. Her name was Mrs. Jacqueline Bouvier Kennedy Onassis. My goal is to one day be as elegant as she was." Lucy pauses. "Your speech impressed me because your words came out perfectly. You managed to get through the first part of your speech without me ever noticing you had a speech impediment. That's determination and dedication young lady. And that's what my son sees in you."

"You've always been my favorite teacher but speaking in front of people will always be my greatest fear. And Jenny Taylor will always be my enemy."

Three days later, I walk into the theater room at Mercy Mansion and sit in a black recliner next to him.

"Did you read my mind?" he asks. "I was thinking about you."

"I thought I'd come see how you're doing."

"You saved me." He's lost in his thoughts.

"What are you thinking about?"

"The moment I proposed to you."

"And boy, was that a mistake!"

It's the longest stare of dislike I've ever received from him. "I've never regretted it. And I'll never forget it." His smile touches his eyes. "It was in this room where I proposed to you." He re-enacts the proposal by kneeling in front of me. "Jacqueline Classie Jones, you're the most beautiful woman in the world. I'm presenting a red single rose to you to remind you that out of a dozen roses this one was the best, just like you. Will you please be my wife?"

"And I took your rose and said yes."

"I planted on your finger a diamond above all diamonds. A three-carat princess cut diamond ring." His voice sounds sad. He stands and returns to his seat. "I'm returning to training camp tomorrow."

My anger peeks. "Is your destiny death?" I stand and storm out of the theater room.

He chases after me.

We stand outside Mercy Mansion.

"What do you want?" he asks.

"I want you to stop giving your life to football."

He pulls me in and tightly holds me. "I can't give you what you want. My first love was football. I can't change that."

Jenny Taylor

Taylor Dairy is a one hundred head free stall dairy that sits on two hundred acres. The last time I visited the dairy was the summer that I turned nine years old.

Jenny Taylor's grandmother appears at the door after I knock. "May I help you?"

"Hi, Susan, it's been a while since I've been here. I'm Classie Jones."

"Oh, my dear, it has been a while. How have you been sweet girl?"

"I'm not well."

She steps out onto the front porch. "Would you like to come in? I can pour you some sweet, iced tea."

"Sweet, iced tea sounds perfect," I reply, "but I'd rather sit out here on the porch swing if that's okay with you."

"That's fine by me. I'll prepare your tea."

It's hot and I begin to sweat. But as I sit quietly, I'm reminded of the many times Jenny and I would sit on the porch swing as little girls.

We enrolled in Caldwell Elementary school when we were five. I was a shy little girl, and Jenny was an outspoken one. We were opposites, but somehow, we still became best friends.

I smile when I see an old, crumpled up swimming pool in the front yard. I remembered Susan filling up a plastic swimming pool for us to play in.

"Here, sweet girl, drink up," Susan says as the front door swings open.

"Thank you. I appreciate the tea. But the reason I stopped by was to see Jenny," I reply and then sip the tea. "Is she here?"

"Yes. I'll go get her."

Her blonde hair is pulled back into a ponytail. She's wearing no makeup. She's still slender, and she's rocking a tank top and Daisy Duke shorts. She glares at me and gently closes the screen door.

"Would you like to swing with me?" I ask and pat the spot beside me.

Jenny moves in and sits next to me. "I'm surprised to see you here."

I clear my throat. "I've had some time to figure some things out. It's been a year since I heard about…"

"Me riding your husband hard," she replies with a smirk.

Her dig hurts. "Actually, I believe he was my ex-husband." I attempt to remain cordial. "Do you want some sweet, iced tea?"

"No. What I want is for you to stop acting like nothing has happened between us. We haven't been friends for years."

"At one time, you were my best friend. All of that changed our fifth-grade year. But I don't understand why."

She jumps off the swing. I hurry to steady it. "I don't want to talk to you. It's too hard for me. Our fifth-grade year was terrible. And recalling it will only bring me more pain."

I walk towards her and lean against the porch railing. "Terrible for you, it was terrible for me. You made my life hell throughout school. You bullied me because I had a speech impediment."

"Poor, Classie," she mocks and invades my space. "Now get the hell off this porch!" She pushes me over the rails, and I land on my back.

But I quickly get up to dust myself off. "Look here! I'm not that ten-year-old little girl you mocked in the fifth grade. I'm not that sixteen-year-old teenager you mocked in the hallways. I'm not that twenty-five-year-old woman that bawled her eyes out when I heard the love of my life slept with you. I've lived through hell the last three years. But no more! I'm a fighter and I came to fight. I came to face one of the demons that took my joy from me. That demon is you!"

"But I admitted that I slept with Jake. What more do you want from me?"

"I want an apology and an explanation! Why did you bully me in school?"

She snickers under her breath.

"Jenny, if you want to continue to live like hell, it's your choice. Go ahead and keep running through the burning fire while the demons continue to chase you. They'll not stop tormenting you until you stop, turn, and face them. But I'll no longer run from them. I'm standing firm. The fire around me is being extinguished today. I'm walking through it. You have a choice. You can stay and let it consume you forever, or Jenny, you can take my hand and walk through it with me."

She takes my hand and together we sit on the steps of the porch.

"I'm sorry for the way I treated you throughout school. But I was dealing with so much pain." She looks at me with pained eyes. "Max raped me when I was a little girl. I was embarrassed to tell my grandmother. I felt dirty like the trash that he said I was. My grandmother loved him. She was all that I had, and I didn't want her to leave me like my mother did." She begins to weep and leans her head against my shoulder.

"It's okay. Crying allows you to release the pain. It's healthy to face the truth." I wait for her to stop crying before I ask, "But why did you bully me, when I was your best friend?"

"I was mad at you because you stopped coming to my house to play with me. Max wouldn't touch me when you were around."

I gently wipe a tear off her cheek. "Oh, Jenny, when Max spanked me with a switch because we made mud pies with his goat's milk, I wasn't allowed to come back over. But we invited you to my house a million times."

"I felt like trash. And trash didn't belong at Jones Ranch."

"I wish I'd known the reason you wouldn't come over. My parents loved you. My father made me pray for you. You're not trash either. Max's voice is in your head telling you that."

She stares at the green rolling hills. "I'm sorry that I slept with Jake. He had a party celebrating his new career as a paramedic. But he was on pain medication from his prior injury when we slept together. He regretted sleeping with me. We haven't spoken since. And that's the truth."

I look at my phone. "Jenny, I've got to catch a plane. Brett Rainey is expecting me at the San Antonio airport."

"I heard about you and Rainey. Does he make you happy?"

"I think so."

She walks me to my truck and embraces me. "Thank you for listening to me. You've come along way. I can tell by the way you speak that you've overcome your speech disorder. I hope that you will find a way to forgive me."

"I have forgiven you. You're a beautiful woman created by God. That makes you, his daughter. You're not trash. You're royalty. Thank you for allowing me to confront my demon."

She kisses me on the cheek. "Take care, Sassy Classie."

The Ride

He greets me at the San Antonio airport in a white button-down shirt, cowboy jeans and boots.

"Did you go country on me why I was gone?"

He loads my luggage inside the back of his new pickup truck. "I purchased a horse and thought we could ride him today," he replies and opens the passenger side door.

I look at his shoulder. "I told you it would be better."

"Yes. And we need to talk about that."

Rainey opens the gate, and I follow him through a twelve stall, raised center aisle, red metal barn.

I look up. "Skylights in a barn?"

"That's for star gazing."

"And the mattress in the corner?"

"That's for a romp in the hay."

"I will not sleep with a man until marriage." I lean against the barn door and watch him lead a horse out. He gently places a red saddle pad on its back. I notice a brown leather saddle sitting in the corner of the barn near the mattress. I check the straps to make sure they'll be secure. I tie off the strap, secure the cinches, and clip the breast collar by the side of the stirrup.

"Do you want me to saddle him?" Rainey asks.

"Nope. I've saddled horses a billion times. You stay right there." Standing next to the horse, I hold the saddle on my hip. I rock it up onto the horse's back. I slide it into place and adjust the pad. "Would you like to connect the cinches?" I ask Rainey.

"Nope. I'm enjoying the view," he replies looking at my backside.

I finish connecting the cinches and then connect the breast collar. "It's time to cowboy up!"

He places his left leg in the stirrup and lifts his right leg over. I follow suit and place my arms around his waist.

The estate has plenty of wildflowers. We gallop through them and then tie the horse off at a tree at a nearby pond.

Rainey removes his shirt. "Sorry. But it's hot out here."

My eyes devour his profile. "Don't be sorry on my account."

He laughs and retrieves a blanket from the saddle bag. He spreads it out under the tree. He removes his socks and boots. I take my sandals off and toss them nearby. He watches me walk towards the pond. "Where are you going?"

I remove my white cotton dress and leave him staring at me in my undergarments. "To cool off."

"So how is Jake Mercy? I heard he recovered pretty fast."

"Nothing that my touch couldn't handle."

He stares at me in disbelief. "You've got to explain that to me."

"Perhaps another time," I reply and wade into the pond.

Rainey's taking a shower and cleaning up in his master suite while I sit on his bed reading. He returns to me wearing a t-shirt and jeans. His hair is damp, and his cologne is strong. "It is your turn. I placed your luggage in the bathroom."

The hot water pours over my body pleasuring my skin. I smell the shampoo first before applying it to my hair. It smells like Rainey. I search for women's shampoo, but I find none, so I use his. I complete my shower with men's body wash before stepping out to dry off.

I pull a white crop top, white panties, a matching bra, and a short pair of light blue ripped shorts from my luggage. I towel dry my hair and return to Rainey, who is sitting in the living room watching his gigantic television. With my hands on my hips, I stand in front of it.

He gazes at my belly button. "Did your father approve that piercing?"

"I don't run all my decisions by him. There are some things better left unknown."

He gestures for me to join him on the couch. "I'd like for you to tell me more about your family. Obviously, I know your father is John Jones, the megachurch pastor, and your mother is Julie Jones, a well-liked realtor and interior decorator. What else is there to know about your family?"

I prop my legs up on his white ottoman. "My sister is Norma Peterson Jones. She's married to an attorney. And she was a wild child growing up."

"And now?"

"I think she's having an affair with a local country music singer. But she hasn't confirmed that to me yet. Her dream is to sing country, but right now, she plays piano and sings at my father's church."

"Do you like attending your father's church?"

I remove my hair from its messy bun and allow it to fall over my shoulders. "I love my father. We were extremely close, but when Mercy and I divorced, and I moved here last fall, I forgot about his church and church in general."

He looks at me with admiration. "But I sense you're a good person. You like to abide by the rules."

"Most of the time. I try to remain sober for the gift to work. But lately it's been hard to do."

"That's why you refrain from alcohol?"

I retrieve the remote from his hand and turn up the television to distract him from talking about my gift. Jocelyn Maverick James is talking about the Dallas Wranglers and Mercy's return to training camp. "Jocelyn Maverick James. She's insanely beautiful. But when did she make her comeback? I thought she was covering high school sports."

"Do we have to talk about her?"

"I apologize. But I'd like to know what it's like playing for the Texas Royal Sports Family?"

He doesn't look amused. "Why don't you ask Jake Mercy what it's like playing for them?"

"Because I'm not dating Mercy. I'm dating you. I'm not asking Mercy about his experience with them; I'm asking you about yours."

He collects his thoughts. "I owe my career to Wrangler and Lilly James. I love playing for them. They've always treated me like family. But I'm not a fan of Jackson Maverick or his daughter. I'm glad I don't play for the Houston Torpedoes."

"Do you like Jasper?"

He cuts his eyes at me. "I told you he's the youngest general manager in baseball history. I respect him."

"Then how do you feel about him trying to sign Luke Ford?"

He glances at me with enthusiasm. "You've done your baseball homework."

I offer him my best smile. "I happen to have a crush on a baseball player. I had no choice."

He kisses my forehead. "I'm sorry if I sounded annoyed with you earlier. And Luke Ford is a beast. He's one of the best pitchers to ever play the game. But he won't sign with the Dallas Wardens. He'll sign with the Houston Torpedoes. Jackson Maverick will not settle for anything but the best."

"But you said you are the best."

He laughs. "If I'm healthy, I'm the best. And thanks to you, I'm healthy. In fact, my arm is stronger than it has ever been. And since we are discussing baseball, I'd like to run something by you." He peers at me with his gorgeous eyes. "I'd like you to move in here. I know you live in a small apartment, and I could use someone watching the place while I'm living in Southlake. I rented it for a year."

"You do realize I come from a wealthy family, don't you? Like you, I have a healthy bank account. I choose to live in a small apartment."

"I know. But I'd like for you to live here."

"But I have plans to move back to Tye soon. The Tye Gazette has offered me a job. How long do I have to think about it?"

"Two days. I'm returning to baseball in two days."

My mind drifts to Jake Mercy. The longer I stay away from Tye and Mercy, the easier it'll be to completely let go. "I would love to live in your fortress. However, I'd love to travel to Dallas and watch you play."

"And I'd love for you to come watch me play."

Norma Jenna Jones

It is September. I pack up my father's pickup with fishing gear and report to the pond to fish with him.

"I think I got a keeper," I say and reel in a bass.

"But what are you going to do with it?"

"Are we talking about this bass or Brett Rainey?"

Dad helps me cut the bass from the line. "Brett Rainey."

"He's been on the road so much; I hardly see him. I now know why I hate baseball so much; baseball has more games than football," I reply and place my pole on the tailgate.

"Have you revealed your secret to him?"

"It was hard to reveal it to you. I saw the disappointment in your eyes. How am I supposed to tell him that I slept with Mercy?"

"It was before y'all began dating." He folds up his folding chair. "I have loved you no matter what. And Rainey will, too. But he deserves to hear the truth."

Dad and I return to the main house for lunch, but we walk into a screaming match between Norma and Tony.

"Why are you screaming at my sister?"

Tony's livid. "Tell her!"

I look at my father out of the corner of my eye and grimace. His face is red, but he remains silent.

Norma gestures for me to sit at the kitchen table. "You're not going to like what I have to say, but I had a procedure done two weeks ago. It required a follow-up today."

"A procedure I knew nothing about," Tony says.

"What type of procedure?" I ask worried.

"I found out that I was pregnant."

I smile with joy. "That's great news. I'll be an aunt." But then I frown. "Wait a minute. I thought that Tony wasn't able to have children?"

"I can't! The child wasn't mine. Your sister had an affair and even worse she had an abortion."

The word abortion bounces off my broken heart like a boomerang. "This is a joke, right? Tell me you didn't?"

"It was her decision," Mom says.

"Are y'all going to accept this behavior? This is unacceptable," I say to my parents.

"It's my life, not yours. I had a right to choose. I had a pregnancy that I didn't want."

Tony murmurs something under his breath before he says, "John and Julie, I'm sorry for the drama that my wife has caused this family. Classie, I'm sorry that you lost a child and had to learn that your sister has no respect for life or for marriage. And Norma, I'll have divorce papers drawn up tomorrow." He storms out of the kitchen.

Norma weeps, mascara running down her cheeks.

"You're right. It's your life, not mine. But you'll be held accountable for the blood that you shed. I'm not upset that you had an affair. In fact, I assumed it was happening. But the pregnancy exposed your sin. And instead of you reaping what you sowed, you disposed of the consequence."

Her tears are uncontrollable.

"We have conflicting beliefs in this room. Norma made her decision and it's finished. Classie, it wasn't your decision to make. We're family. We'll act accordingly. It's in times like these that we must stick together," Mom says.

"Mom. This isn't a bad decision that Norma made like the time she drove home drunk. Or the time she was busted for having a boyfriend in her bed. Or the time she got caught with marijuana in her room. This was a life. A life she created with someone she loved or possibly loved. Unfortunately for him, she was married to Tony."

It's dark as I travel down a winding country road thinking about my sister's abortion. There's only one human that would understand what I'm feeling; I call Lucy for his address and travel to Southlake.

With sweaty palms, I ring the doorbell.

A redhead in a t-shirt and panties answers, "May I help you?"

I assume it's another one of his one-night stands. "Does Jake Mercy live here?"

"Yes, but he's in the shower."

I retrieve my phone from my back pocket. "It's midnight. I'm sorry. I shouldn't had come here so late."

"No worries. He played Monday night football. He's still awake."

"Classie. Is that you?" he asks, strolling down the stairs in a towel.

I bite my nail. "Yep. But I apologize. I should go."

Mercy looks at the redhead. "Britt, can you give us a minute?"

"Absolutely."

His blue eyes are gentle. "Something must be wrong. You'd never show up uninvited. It's out of character for you. Why don't you come inside?"

I step inside the foyer. "It's Norma. I just found out that she had an abortion."

"But Tony can't have children."

"I know. She had an affair."

He hears the pain in my voice. "She probably panicked. Maybe she didn't think it through."

"I can't forgive her for this."

"Classie, you're a Christian, you must show your sister some mercy. It's the right thing to do. It's not your place to judge her. It's your place to love her through this. If the shoe were on the other foot, what would you have Norma do?"

He's right. I would ask her to support me. "I'm sorry I interrupted your evening. But thanks for listening." I fixate my eyes on his bare chest. I blush.

"Not a problem. But about this evening. I played the best game of my life against Washington."

"I'm glad."

"Are you?"

"Nope. Not really. I wish Washington would have won."

His smile touches his eyes. "You were right when you said I keep having sex with women to fill a void in my life."

The redhead appears at the top of the staircase. "Are you coming to bed?"

Mercy opens the door for me. "I'm going upstairs to get dressed. I'll meet you at your truck in a few minutes. Give me a minute to send her home."

He asks me to drive him to Tye Town to the football field.

"This brings back some memories," he says as we sit in the bleachers.

"I love being here," I reply and gaze at the scoreboard.

"Why are you home? I didn't know you were in town. If I'd known, I'd given you tickets to the game against Washington."

I hesitate before I reply, "I haven't seen Rainey in a month. I thought I'd watch his game tomorrow night." I look at my phone. "It's one a.m. So, he actually plays tonight."

We see the flashing lights pull into the parking lot as the police officer approaches us with a flashlight.

"Well, if it isn't Officer Willis," I say with a laugh.

"Classie Jones."

"Hi, Ryan. Jake Mercy and I thought it would be fun to share some high school memories."

"The Jake Mercy?" he asks.

"The one and only," Mercy replies and shakes his hand.

"Classie and I were co-workers at the police department while you were off playing college ball in Lubbock." He lowers the flashlight. "I heard you're a dispatcher in San Antonio?"

"I was."

"Was?" Mercy asks.

"I quit my job about three months ago. I've been house sitting in San Antonio for Brett Rainey. But I'm moving back to Tye."

"Then you should come and work with me again. We are hiring dispatchers."

I give him a hug. "Thanks for the offer, but I'll be working at Tye Gazette. You stay safe!"

It's sunset when we return to Mercy's neighborhood. "You look exhausted and pale," Mercy says when we pull into his driveway. "Are you sick? If so, why don't you come in and get some rest for a few hours?"

I laugh. "Heavens no. I'll end up wearing America's team again. And I have a baseball game I must attend this evening, as well as an after party."

The Secret

I'm hoping Rainey won't be able to hide his carnal desires for me. I'm wearing a nude crop top, blue jeans with rips in the thighs, and nude toe pumps. My hair is flat ironed straight, and my makeup is that of a bronze Goddess. I've agreed to meet him at the club instead of waiting for him at the clubhouse. But I'm running late.

Right off I know this is the hot spot for Dallas luxury clubbing. The club has a beautiful gold and red interior with an awesome sound and light system. I pass by numerous V.I.P. lounging sections, as I'm escorted by a blonde waitress to Rainey's reserved spot.

He looks cool and casual in a white fitted t-shirt and skinny jeans when we kiss. Afterwards, I follow him to a table where I meet his personal assistant, Penny, who is wearing an alluring white dress with her hair pulled up into a messy bun. She must be in her early twenties. "It's nice to finally meet you, Miss Jones."

Then I meet his attorney, his physical trainer, and his teammate's groupies.

But there's a flashy woman, with silky, blonde hair, in a white outstanding dress that refuses to make eye contact with me. I'm eager to meet her. "I'm Classie Jones," I say as I watch her look at me like I'm a contagious disease.

She smirks. "It's rare for me to meet another woman that Brett's been committed to. He has the tendency to hit it and quit it." She places a diamond ring on the table. "I'm Vivian Abbott Rainey."

"His ex-wife?"

She rolls her eyes at him. "Unfortunately!"

Rainey's jaw clenches. "Vivian, please move along. I didn't invite you here."

But a loud entourage distracts everyone from the awkward encounter between Rainey and Vivian.

"It's Jake Mercy and his girlfriend," Penny says.

I watch Mercy interact with his redhead in a fitted silver t-shirt, stone washed blue jeans, and casual shoes. And finally, we make eye contact.

He approaches our table. "Rainey, I heard y'all won your game tonight. Congratulations. It looks like y'all could make a run for the Championship Series this season." He ignores my presence.

"I sure hope so."

Mercy raises his beer. "To Rainey and the Dallas Wardens," he toasts, "And to me and Brittany Daniels."

She warmly smiles at him and then says, "And to our baby that's on the way!"

I step out onto the balcony and breathe in the morning air. My eyes widen when I feel his arms wrap around my waist.

"Did you sleep well?" Rainey asks.

I turn to meet his gaze. "Your Southlake home is gorgeous. But it was difficult for me to sleep. I wasn't aware that your neighbor is Brittany Daniels."

He stares at me for what seems like forever. "You were upset with their baby news. May I ask why?"

I take his hand and place it on my stomach. "I have a secret I've been keeping from you."

His eyebrows narrow. "It's impossible. We haven't slept together."

"I know. I'm pregnant with Mercy's child."

He pulls his hand away. "You slept with Jake Mercy?"

"It was before we started dating. It was the day I met Mercy at his lake house. I don't know why I slept with him. It was a big mistake."

He looks furious. "Because you still love him!"

"I can't tell him about the pregnancy. I can't make him choose between…"

"You and Brittany." Rainey looks at me with disappointment. "There's breakfast on the table." He takes a step forward and brings his mouth to mine. He pulls away. "I need to know how you feel about me?" His hand moves to my belly. "I'm willing to announce our pregnancy to the world. But only if you love me."

After Rainey calls Marilyn Maverick James to report my pregnancy, I wake up sweaty from a nap on the couch. I stand and walk towards the kitchen for a drink of water to quench my thirst when a severe pain in my stomach strikes. I creep back to the couch and shout, "Rainey! Please come quick. I think I've miscarried."

Dad places yellow roses on a table near my hospital bed. "Has the doctor been in yet?"

I scowl at him. "Yes. Another spontaneous loss."

"I'm sincerely sorry. I know this must be very painful for you."

I raise my eyebrows. I try my best to look unfazed.

Mom unzips her purse and hands me a Sporting It Magazine. "Perhaps this will make you feel better."

I open the page she has marked with a yellow sticky note. I read the article written by Marilyn Maverick James.

Sporting It Magazine

On the Web

By Marilyn Maverick James

Gianna Dawn Perkins, Senator Russell Perkins' daughter, has announced her engagement to Matthew Abbott, the Texas Governor's son. Brett Rainey, the All-star pitcher for the Dallas Wardens, has announced his pregnancy with his girlfriend, Jacqueline Classie Jones. We wish the happy couples the best.

I throw the magazine on the floor.

"Is her engagement not good news?" Mom asks.

"No. She's my best friend, and I had to read the news in a magazine!"

Dad pulls up a chair and stares at me. "Or could it be she heard about your miscarriage and didn't want to bother you with her good news?"

"But I didn't tell her about my pregnancy."

Mom sighs. "I called her with the news."

With twelve beautiful rainbow roses in his hand, he kisses my forehead. I retrieve the flowers to sniff them. "They smell amazing. Thank you, Rainey."

He walks over to the window and looks out. "I hated to meet your parents on these terms."

Near the door, Mercy's voice is loud, "I think it's my damn right!"

"It's important that she recover from her miscarriage without any distractions to give her a chance to carry again," Mom replies.

"It appears you have some company," Rainey says, acknowledging Mercy's presence.

"Do we need to call security?" a nurse asks after Mercy bursts into the room.

"That won't be necessary," I say and then place Rainey's flowers on a side table.

"Why didn't you tell me about our child?" he asks in anger.

I glance at my mother. "Who told him?"

"I told Lucy, and then she told him."

"Will everyone please give me a moment with Mercy?" I ask clearly to my parents and Rainey.

Rainey brushes my hand. "If you need me, I'll be on the other side of that door."

Mercy looks relieved the moment Rainey leaves the room. "Was it his plan or your plan to hide the truth from me?"

"It was my decision not to tell you about the baby. But that doesn't matter now. The baby is gone."

"You didn't think I had a right to know?"

"I didn't know what to do after I found out that Brittany Daniels was pregnant, too."

He sits quietly in the chair next to my bedside. "I've made a complete mess out of things. I wish things had turned out different. I'm sorry that you've lost another child."

"We've lost another child!"

With tears in his eyes, he grasps my hand. "I would have chosen you. I would have chosen to be with you."

I release his hand. "That's why I chose Rainey to be the father of my child and not you. Brittany deserves your devotion."

"But I don't love her. I love you."

"Don't you dare say you love me again. Because that's far from the truth. You divorced me. You slept with my childhood bully after I moved. You sold our home. And you held my first miscarriage against me. Do you hold this one against me, too?" I know how painful it must be for him to hear the truth, but the truth will set us free. "I chose you when I saved your life. And I wanted to be the mother of your child. But that'll never happen for us. That's obvious. And it'll be too painful for me to watch another woman mother your child. What we've shared is over. I choose to be happy. I choose Rainey."

He's agreeable with the truth. "I wish you nothing but the best. Because the best is what you've always deserved. And Brett Rainey is a lucky man."

I weep, as I watch him walk away. And I know it's for the best. But—is he better as a memory?

Please follow Connie Johnson to obtain the release date of *The Knight, the next book in the series. Enjoy a teaser on the next page.*

FB: @Tales from Perfect Pond
IG: @PerfectPondSeries

To support the author please shop her Texas jewelry collection at KaylaandAsher.com. She will also be selling autographed copies of *The Collapse*.

The Knight

With a troubling mind, Jocelyn views her two-piece business suit crumpled up on the floor in Rainey's hotel loft.

"I can't believe you slept with me," she says ashamed.

He stretches out in bed. "You look comfortable in my shirt," he replies with a laugh.

She beams at him with distaste, as he smiles smugly at her.

"Is it true that you despise social media?" she asks, like the daunting professional sportswriter that she used to be.

He rises from bed. "I hate social media."

Her gaze lowers to his boxers. "Would you call yourself a superstar baller off the field?"

"I'm definitely a superstar baller off the field."

She pulls back the sheets and joins him at the floor-to-ceiling windows.

Overlooking Houston, they watch a glorious, new sunrise suffocate the darkness.

"Why did you have sex with me? Aren't you in love with Classie Jones?"

He traces her lips with his fingers. "Those lips are scarlet. They match my scarlet behavior." He leans in and with a back-breaking kiss covers her mouth with his.

Made in the USA
Middletown, DE
07 November 2021